Bubble Gum Monster

Marilyn D. Anderson

illustrated by Estella Hickman

4-7-95

To Jan,

Happy Reading

Marilyn Anderson

Published by Willowisp Press
801 94th Avenue North, St. Petersburg, Florida 33702

Copyright © 1987 by Willowisp Press,
a division of PAGES, Inc.

Printed in the United States of America

10 9 8 7 6 5

ISBN 0-87406-299-3

Contents

Contents

The Bubble Gum Monster

It happened so fast! One minute I was on my bed looking at baseball cards. The next minute my dog Spud started barking. And then someone screamed.

A pair of Dad's undershorts plopped
on my head! I pulled off the
undershorts, and saw my mother
lying across my desk.

"Mother, are you all right?" I cried.

She nodded, but she couldn't get up. It looked like a huge pink monster had her. I couldn't believe it!

"Yes, Sam, I'm fine," she said. "I was just going to put clean clothes in your drawer. But your crazy dog tripped me."

"Then why aren't you getting up?" I wondered.

"I'm stuck," she said.

"Stuck?" I repeated. "I'll help you." I took hold of her shoulders and pulled. And now I could see what she meant.

A monster's thick pink arms were holding on to her.

"Sam," she said angrily. "It's that terrible bubble gum of yours. I told you to get rid of it weeks ago."

"Uh, oh," I said to myself.

You probably think my mother was stuck in some little half-chewed wad of goo. Wrong. We're talking about a HUMONGOUS pile of pink bubble gum. The pile was made of the kind of gum that takes your teeth out when you try to chew it.

Will the Gum Stretch Forever?

My pile got started when I bought my first stack of baseball cards. The cards always come with a piece of gum. I don't like bubble gum, but I couldn't just throw it away. So I put the gum on the corner of my desk.

That was 876 cards ago! My pile of gum was huge now. And the pile seemed to be getting bigger. It was right over a heating register.

The gum was all melted together, gooey and sticky. Stray socks, old tissues, and dead flies were stuck in it. I thought it was neat. Mother had told me to get rid of it. But I hadn't. Now she was stuck in it.

"Hey, I'm sorry," I said. "I promise to throw it all away. But first we have to get you out of this mess."

This time I grabbed Mother around the waist. I counted, "One, two, three!" I pulled as hard as I could. Even Spud tried to help. The gum stretched and stretched. But it wouldn't let go.

Then PLOP. I fell on my bed and let go of my mother. The gum jerked her back. I jumped up and pulled her again. You won't believe what happened next. My sheets and blankets got stuck in the gum.

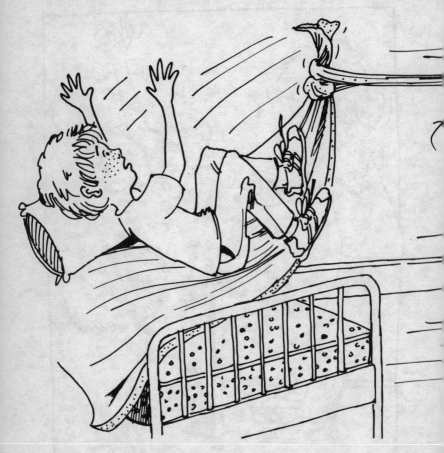

I pulled Mother into the hall. The more I pulled, the more the gum stretched and popped. It took down the picture of Aunt Matilda.

The living room was just ahead. We bumped into an easy chair and knocked over the coffee table.

The gum sucked up magazines, books, couch pillows, and a rubber plant. The gum stretched and crackled. But it didn't break.

I didn't know what to do. So I pulled Mother into the dining room. The gum grabbed the tablecloth. But it still didn't break.

We were in the kitchen now. The gum pulled the magnets off the refrigerator door. It took the pot holders and the pans off the stove. I still couldn't believe what was happening. There was nowhere else to go.

What Am I Going to Do?

Suddenly, I had an idea. I opened the back door and pulled Mother outside toward the big oak tree. I told her to hang onto it. Then I ran back to shut the door.

SNAP! THE GUM BROKE! Spud's hair stood on end. Strands of gum shot into the air. They got tangled in the tree. Mother was surprised. She almost fell. But she held on.

"We did it," I yelled. "You're free!" Spud and I were so happy we did a little dance.

But Mother wasn't happy. She looked down at her gooey hands. She stared at her ruined dress. "Sam, I'm a mess," she said. "And all because of your gum."

"I'm sorry," I said. "I'll get rid of it right now. But . . . but how?"

Mother gave me one of her looks. She thought a moment. "Use rubber gloves," she said. She started for the back door. "Put salad oil on the gloves so the gum won't stick."

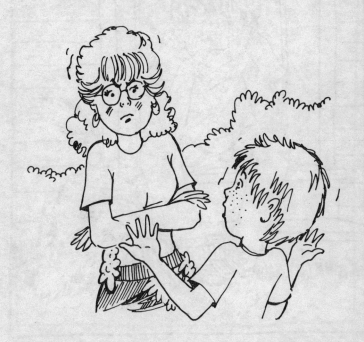

"What about this other stuff that's stuck in it?"

She frowned. "Throw it all away," she said. "I'll expect you to pay for everything out of your own money."

We were at the back door now. She stepped inside. "I'm going to take a shower," she said. "And I don't ever want to see another piece of bubble gum." Then she slammed the door.

The Cleanup

Spud and I looked at each other. Then I opened the door carefully. We looked in. Slowly the gum had started to shrink back to my room. It had taken Spud's dog dish and a rug with it.

I got some rubber gloves. I found the bottle of salad oil. Spud and I tiptoed slowly to my room. We wanted to sneak up on the bubble gum monster.

My room was a mess! The gum and all the stuff it had taken were everywhere. How was I ever going to get it all to the trash cans? I wondered.

I went to the garage and got Dad's wheelbarrow. I put it outside my bedroom window.

I went back inside and put on the rubber gloves. I poured salad oil over them. The wheelbarrow and shovel got a dose, too. Then I began to shovel the gum out the window.

Soon the wheelbarrow was full. I shut the window on the glop, and went outside.

Then I took a deep breath. I tried to move the wheelbarrow. The gum stretched and popped. The wheelbarrow almost tipped over.

But finally the thick goo broke. Long ropes of the bubble gum dragged behind me on the way to the garbage cans. I dumped my load in a can and shut the lid. I made five more trips.

At last the gum was gone. I was so tired I could barely walk. But then I thought of something else. I got some paper and wrote a note. It said,

Dear Garbagemen,
Don't open our cans. Just take them to the dump.

I didn't want that bubble gum monster to get loose again.

5
Stop, Spud! Come Back!

I figured my bubble gum trouble was over. Two days later Spud started barking at the window. I looked out.

A bright green garbage truck stopped in front of our house. Two men in uniforms got out. They read my note.

Spud doesn't like garbagemen. He clawed at the window and barked again. But I was glad to see them. "Good-bye, forever, bubble gum," I said.

The men threw our cans in the back of their truck. They got in the cab. The big trash compactor started up. It hummed and whirred. Then it went *BWONG!*

Spud got all excited about that. I had to find out more, too. I grabbed Spud's leash, and we raced outside.

When we got to the truck, pink goo was oozing from the truck's seams. More pink stuff poured out its back. Spud barked and barked at the truck. A crowd began to gather.

"What happened?" someone yelled.

I knew what was wrong. The pink goo was my bubble gum. It had become warm in the hot sun. It had bubbled up until it broke the truck. Now it was loose. And it was more sticky and gooey than ever.

Just then Spud ran away from me. He was heading for the garbagemen. I covered my eyes. "Stop, Spud! Come back!" I cried.

But Spud never got to the garbagemen. He tried to run through a
sea of bubble gum. But the gooey
mess stuck to his legs. Soon he was
running in slow motion. Finally Spud
couldn't move at all.

"Hey, kid, is that your dog?" asked
one of the garbagemen.

"Yes," I said. "Will you help me get
him out of there?"

"We'd better call the fire department," said the other garbageman.
"They know how to rescue animals."

Firemen to the Rescue

The fire department sent a big hook and ladder truck. Three men arrived wearing red hats. One man's hat said "Chief."

The chief laughed at Spud. The other firemen laughed, too.

"Do something," said the garbage-men.

"Okay," said the chief. "But we don't want to get stuck in the gum. Let's try to pick up the dog from above."

The firemen backed the big hook and ladder truck toward Spud. The ladder stretched over the sea of gum. One of the men crawled out on the ladder. He put his arms around Spud's body.

"Okay," he said. "I'm ready."

"Good work," said the chief. "Let's raise the ladder."

And that's what they did. The ladder, Spud, and the fireman went into the air. "Hang on, Spud," I yelled.

"Hang on, Mike," the other fireman called. "Don't let the bubble gum get you."

Will Spud be Saved?

The gum stretched up and up. Soon it looked like a wide pink circus tent. But it didn't break.

"Back the truck up," said the chief. "See if the gum will let go."

So they moved the truck back. The gum formed a thick pink rope, but it didn't break.

"More," said the chief. The truck moved back again. The pink rope got thinner. I could feel my heart beat faster. Boy, Spud really looked scared.

"Now, lower the ladder," said the chief. The truck lowered Spud and the fireman to the ground.

"All right, boys," said the chief. "Cut the dog loose." The fireman attacked the gum with an ax. Soon Spud was free.

I rushed over and kissed Spud on the nose. But I didn't hug him because he was too gooey.

"Thank you," I told the firemen. "Thank you for saving my dog. But how will I ever get the gum off him?"

The chief scratched his head. "That's a good question," he said. "I guess you'll have to cut it off."

I sighed. "Spud sure won't like that."

8

My Dog, Spud

The firemen left and I tied Spud to a tree. I got some scissors and started cutting. Spud tried to get away. But I kept cutting.

Finally the gum was gone. The fur on Spud's legs and back was gone, too. He looked like a lion. But he was lots funnier. I couldn't keep from laughing.

Well, Spud really hated his haircut.
He put his tail between his legs. He
crouched down and ran to the back
door. I followed him to my room
where he crawled under my bed.

"I'm sorry I laughed at you," I told him. "But I hope you've learned a lesson, Spud. Never run out to the garbagemen again. And I promise I won't save another HUMONGOUS pile of bubble gum."

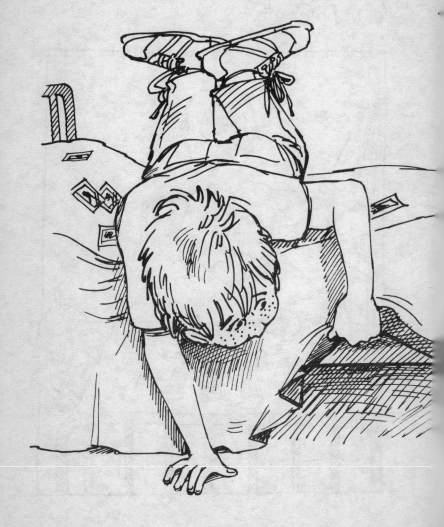

Well, I didn't expect Spud to answer me. But I did hear something. It sounded like chewing. And it was coming from under my bed. Slowly, I pulled up the bedspread and looked under.

"Spud, you crazy dog!" I yelled. "Leave that piece of bubble gum alone!"

The End

About the Author

MARILYN D. ANDERSON grew up on a dairy farm in Minnesota. On the farm she learned to love animals. Many of her books are about training and caring for horses and other animals.

Mrs. Anderson is a former music teacher. She taught band and choir for seventeen years. Her favorite instruments were drums and the violin.

Now she stays busy training young horses and riding in dressage shows. She works at a library, gives piano lessons, and, of course, writes books.

Other books by Marilyn D. Anderson include *The Horse That Came to Breakfast*, *Hot Fudge Pickles*, and *We Have to Get Rid of These Puppies!*

Mrs. Anderson and her husband live in Bedford, Indiana.